Timmy plays Football

EGMONT

First Published in Great Britain in 2010
by Egmont UK Limited
239 Kensington High Street, London W8 6SA

The sun was shining on the Nursery playing fields. All the little animals were wide-eyed with excitement. Today they were going to play football!

TOOT! TOOT!

Osbourne blew his referee's whistle.

Meanwhile, Timmy was playing with a football, dribbling the ball along like a real footballer.

BAAH! BAAH!

Timmy loved football!

TOOT! TOOT! Osbourne blew his whistle again, this time a little louder.

Paxton oinked in delight. Ruffy and Otus were so excited they could not keep still!

TOOWIT! TOOWOO!

Otus was paying close attention to Osbourne.

Timmy found his place in line with the other little animals and was clutching the football under his arm.

Osbourne nodded at the little animals and signalled to Timmy to let go of the football. Timmy blinked at Osbourne, he wanted to keep the ball.

BAAH! BAAH!

Timmy clung on to the football.

Otus waddled up to Timmy. He took the ball and passed it back to Osbourne.

Osbourne nodded his head in approval and Otus returned to the line-up.

Osbourne clapped his wings to get the little animals' attention, calling Ruffy to step forward from the line.

Ruffy looked down at the football at his feet, he did not know what to do. Puzzled, Ruffy did not kick the ball, instead he picked up the ball in his mouth and shook it.

Osbourne shook his head and pointed at his foot. Ruffy dropped the ball and kicked it, the ball scuttled towards the goal post.

Next it was Paxton's turn to shoot for the goal.

OINK! OINK!

Paxton could not wait to have a go.

TOOT! TOOT!

Went Osbourne's whistle.

Paxton shuffled up to the ball, kicking it towards the goal. The ball rolled up to the post and landed in front of Osbourne.

Meanwhile, Timmy was jumping from hoof to hoof. He knew he could score a goal.

It was Otus' turn to kick the ball next.
Osbourne passed the ball to Otus, who stepped
away as it rolled towards him.

TOOWIT! TOOWOO!

Osbourne showed Otus how to shoot
for the goal.

Instead, Otus picked up the ball and waddled
towards the goal, handing it back to Osbourne.

Osbourne peeped his whistle and
patted Otus on the head.

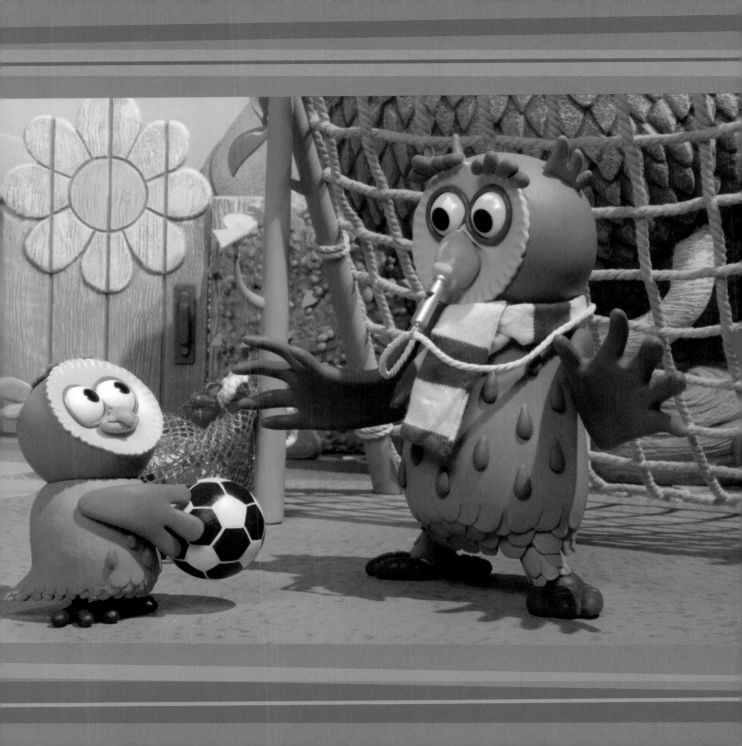

Finally, it was Timmy's turn, he could
not wait to score a goal!

BAAH! BAAH!

Timmy cried. Instead of kicking the ball, he threw
it up into the air, bouncing it up and down.
Otus stared in amazement at Timmy.

Timmy kicked the ball as hard as he could.
All the little animals watched as the ball sailed
through the air and landed with a splash
in the water trough.

Timmy did a little jig to celebrate his
SUPER-KICK!

Osbourne sighed and let the whistle drop
from his beak, turning around to see Timmy
with the ball again.

BAAH! BAAH!

Timmy was dribbling the ball with Otus
waddling behind him.

TOOT! TOOT!

Osbourne blew his whistle hard, giving Timmy
such a fright he headed the ball high into the air.
The ball bounced on the ground and rolled
towards Otus, who picked it up
and gave it back to Osbourne.

Osbourne sighed and picked up the ball, this football game was not going very well.

The little animals followed Osbourne into the playing field and they watched him set some flowerpots on the ground in a row.

OINK! OINK!

Paxton was very excited.

What were they going to play now?
All the little animals were puzzled and stared intently at Osbourne.

TOOT! TOOT!

Osbourne blew his whistle and everyone stood to attention.

BAAH! BAAH!

Timmy could not wait to get the ball again.

Osbourne took the ball and showed the little animals how to dribble it in and out and around the flowerpots.

PHEW! Osbourne puffed, out of breath!

Timmy was the first to have a go.

BAAH! BAAH!

Timmy was off, running in completely the wrong direction, dribbling the ball as fast as he could.

Timmy was having so much fun, he had forgotten all about the flowerpots, he was running and dribbling and running and dribbling!

The class were jumping up and down, they cheered in amazement at Timmy.

He was **VERY** good at dribbling.

Osbourne blew his whistle, finally Timmy stopped.
He sighed and passed the ball to Otus.

Otus was still puzzled. He looked at the
ball, picked it up and waddled towards
the flowerpots.

Otus waddled in and out of the flowerpots,
carrying the ball very carefully!

Timmy bounded towards poor Otus and took
the ball. Otus stood very still in shock.

TOOT! TOOT! went the whistle.
Timmy bowed his head and gave the
ball back to Osbourne.

Just then the cuckoo popped
out of the clock – nap time!
All the little animals ran to the Nursery,
except Timmy, who followed them slowly
carrying the football under his arm!

The little animals settled down for their nap.
Timmy lay down on the floor using the football as
a pillow, all that running and dribbling had made
him **VERY** tired.

Osbourne and Harriet watched on, shaking
their heads fondly at Timmy as he snoozed.

It wasn't long before the cuckoo popped out of the clock again – playtime! Everyone ran into the Nursery courtyard. Timmy followed still clutching the football! Now all he needed was someone to play with.

Ruffy and Paxton were busy playing on the roundabout. Mittens and Yabba were busy playing catch. Timmy sat down, nobody wanted to play football.

Otus dropped his book and waddled over to Timmy with the football. Otus wanted to play!

Timmy kicked the ball to Otus, who picked up the football and gave it back to him. Timmy sighed, he lifted his little hoof and showed Otus how to kick the ball. Soon, they were passing the ball back and forth, having lots of fun!

Otus kicked the ball hard. Everyone watched in amazement as it landed right in the goal! The little animals cheered and clapped at Otus' goal.

Timmy and Otus jumped up and down! Timmy realised that teaching his friend was much more fun than playing on his own!